I'M JUST LIKE MY MOM
ME PAREZCO TANTO A MI MAMÁ

By Jorge Ramos

Illustrated by Akemi Gutiérrez

rayo

An Imprint of HarperCollins Publishers

For my mom and my dad, because I am so much like them.
For my sister, Lourdes, and for my brothers, Alejandro,
Eduardo, and Gerardo, because we are so similar to each other.
For my daughter, Paola, and my son, Nicolás,
because they are so much like me.

—J.R.

For Sam Luft and his little sister Maegan

—A.G.

Rayo is an imprint of HarperCollins Publishers.
I'm Just Like My Mom / I'm Just Like My Dad: Me parezco tanto a mi mamá / Me parezco tanto a mi papá
Text copyright © 2008 by Jorge Ramos   Illustrations copyright © 2008 by Akemi Gutiérrez
Manufactured in China.
Library of Congress Cataloging-in-Publication Data is available.
ISBN 978-0-06-123968-7 (trade bdg.)

Designed by Stephanie Bart-Horvath
16 SCP 10 9
❖
First Edition

My mom has long hair like mine,
and we both have green eyes like Grandma's.

Mi mamá tiene el pelo largo como el mío,
y las dos tenemos los ojos verdes como los de la abuela.

When I'm mad, my forehead wrinkles just like my mom's.

Cuando me enojo, arrugo la frente igual que mi mamá.

And when I sneeze, I sneeze loudly,
just like my mom.

Y cuando estornudo, se escucha muy fuerte,
igual que cuando lo hace mi mamá.

My mom likes to listen to my music, and I like wearing her bracelets and shoes.

A mi mamá le gusta escuchar mi música y a mí me gusta ponerme sus pulseras y sus zapatos.

My mom and I like to write letters to our family and friends. We both like to draw pictures on our letters, too.

A mi mamá y a mí nos gusta escribirle cartas a nuestra familia y a nuestros amigos. Y a las dos nos gusta ponerles dibujos a las cartas.

When I ask my mom, "Who do I look like?" she gives me a mirror and says that she can see our whole family on my face.

Cuando le pregunto a mi mamá: "¿A quién me parezco?", ella me pone frente al espejo y me dice que puede ver a toda nuestra familia en mi cara.

Then I look in the mirror and I know that I'll never be alone.

Por eso, cuando me veo en el espejo, sé que nunca estaré sola.

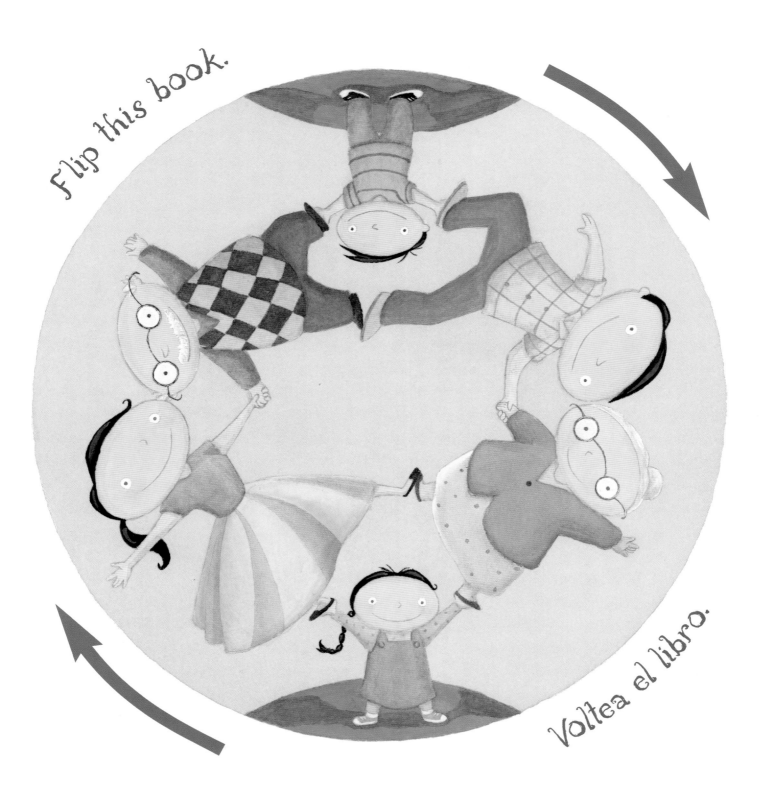

Flip this book.

Voltea el libro.

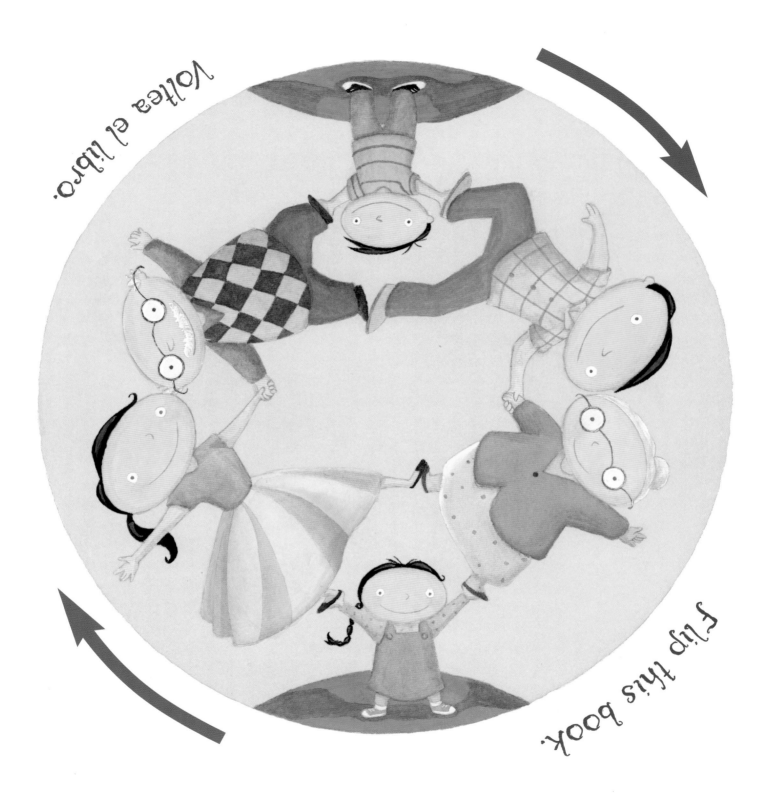

Voltea el libro.

Flip this book.

Por eso, cuando me veo en el espejo sé que nunca estaré solo.

Then I look in the mirror and I know that I'll never be alone.

Cuando le pregunto a mi papá: "¿A quién me parezco?", él me pone frente al espejo y me dice que puede ver a toda nuestra familia en mi cara.

When I ask my dad, "Who do I look like?" he gives me a mirror and says that he can see our whole family on my face.

A mi papá y a mí nos gusta leer antes de irnos a dormir.
A veces, leemos sobre lugares que quedan muy lejos.

My dad and I like reading before we go to sleep.
Sometimes we read about faraway places.

Y por las tardes, mi papá juega al fútbol conmigo.

And in the afternoon my dad plays soccer with me.

When we drink hot chocolate together in the morning, I get a mustache just like my dad's.

Cuando tomamos chocolate caliente por la mañana, se me forma un bigote igual que el de mi papá.

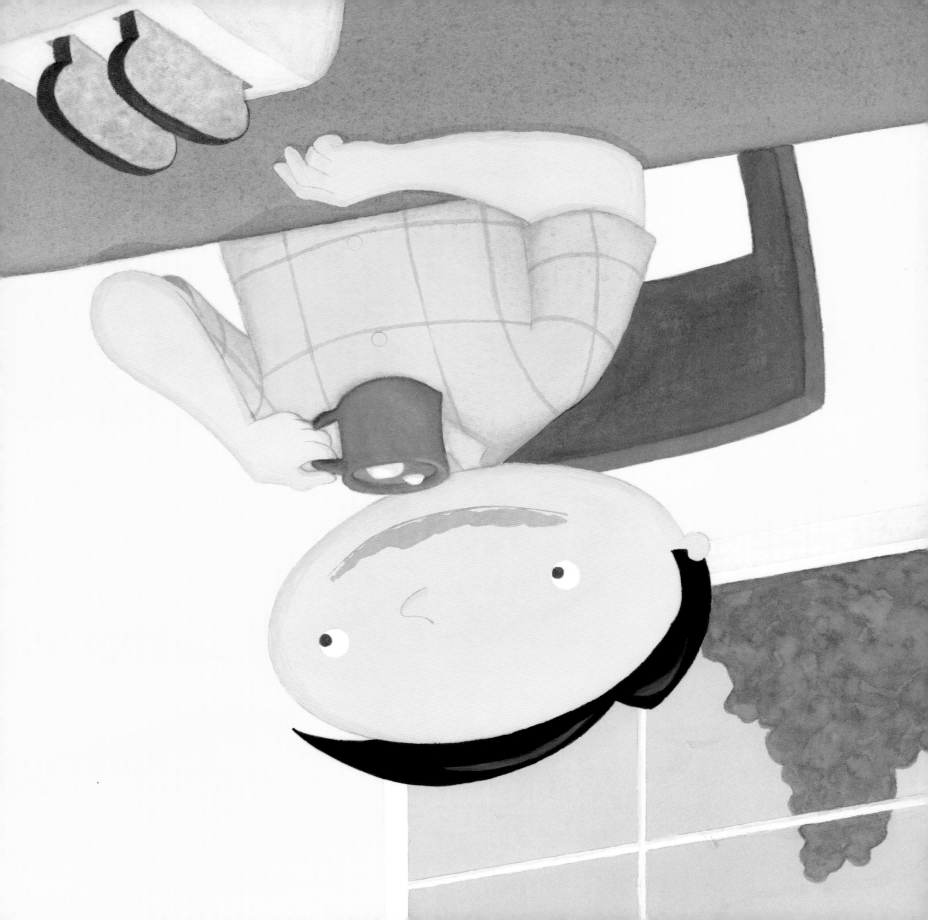

Yo duermo boca abajo, igual que mi papá, y a los
dos nos gusta despertarnos bien temprano.

I sleep facedown, just like my dad, and we both like to get up early in the morning.

My dad has long legs like mine,
and we both have Grandpa's pointy nose.

Mi papá tiene las piernas largas como las mías,
y los dos tenemos la misma nariz puntiaguda del abuelo.

I'M JUST LIKE MY DAD
ME PAREZCO TANTO A MI PAPÁ

Por Jorge Ramos

Ilustrado por Akemi Gutiérrez

rayo

Una rama de HarperCollins Publishers

The Adventures of TAXI DOG

by Debra and Sal Barracca
pictures by Mark Buehner

PUFFIN BOOKS

PUFFIN BOOKS
Published by the Penguin Group
Penguin Putnam Books for Young Readers, 345 Hudson Street, New York, New York 10014, U.S.A.
Penguin Books Ltd, 27 Wrights Lane, London W8 5TZ, England
Penguin Books Australia Ltd, Ringwood, Victoria, Australia
Penguin Books Canada Ltd, 10 Alcorn Avenue, Toronto, Ontario, Canada M4V 3B2
Penguin Books (N.Z.) Ltd, 182-190 Wairau Road, Auckland 10, New Zealand

Penguin Books Ltd, Registered Offices: Harmondsworth, Middlesex, England

First published in the United States of America by Dial Books for Young Readers, a division of Penguin Books USA Inc., 1990
Published by Puffin Books. a member of Penguin Putnam Books for Young Readers. 2000

32 33 34 35 36 37 38 39 40

THE LIBRARY OF CONGRESS HAS CATALOGED THE DIAL EDITION AS FOLLOWS:
Barracca, Debra. The adventures of Taxi Dog/by Debra and Sal Barracca;
pictures by Mark Buehner.
p. cm.
Summary: A stray dog in New York City is adopted by a taxi driver, with whom he thereafter rides and shares adventures each day.
ISBN 0-8037-0671-5. ISBN 0-8037-0672-3 [lib. bdg.]
[1. Dogs—Fiction. 2. Taxicabs—Fiction. 3. New York (N.Y.)—Fiction. 4. City and town life—Fiction. 5. Stories in rhyme.]
I. Barracca, Sal. II. Buehner, Mark, ill. III. Title.
PZ8.3.B25263Ad 1990 [E]—dc19 89-1056 CIP AC
Puffin Books ISBN 978-0-14-056665-9

Manufactured in China

For all the homeless and abused creatures of the world—
may they all find peace some day.
D.B. and S.B.

To Mom and Dad
M.B.

My name is Maxi,
I ride in a taxi
Around New York City all day.
I sit next to Jim,
(I belong to him),
But it wasn't always this way.

I grew up in the city,
    All dirty and gritty,
        Looking for food after dark.
I roamed all around,
    Avoiding the pound,
        And lived on my own in the park.

One day a car stopped—
    Its tire had popped.
        Out stepped a tall man, I could see.
He came over and said
    As he patted my head,
        "Are you lost? You can come home with me!"

Did I hear right? Oh, boy!
My tail wagged with joy—
I jumped right up on the seat!
He said, "My name's Jim,"
I could ride home with him
And he'd give me some good food to eat.

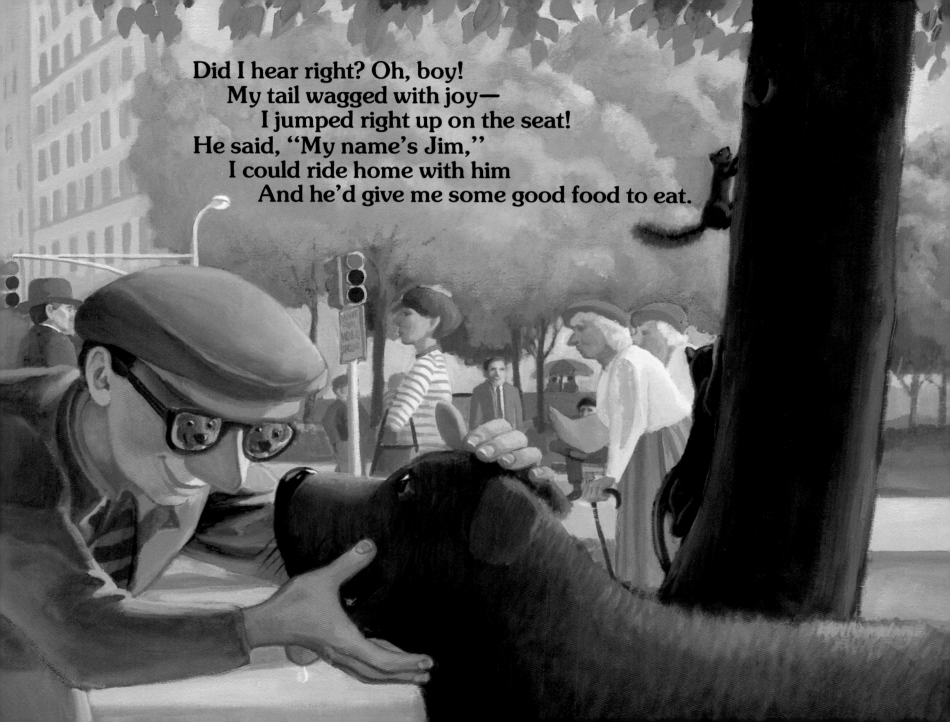

I ate and I ate,
        I cleaned the whole plate.
                Then Jim took a scarf of bright red.
He tied it around me,
        So glad that he found me,
                And kissed me on top of my head.

My wish had come true—
I would start life anew.
At last I had a warm home
With someone to love me
And take good care of me—
No longer would I have to roam.

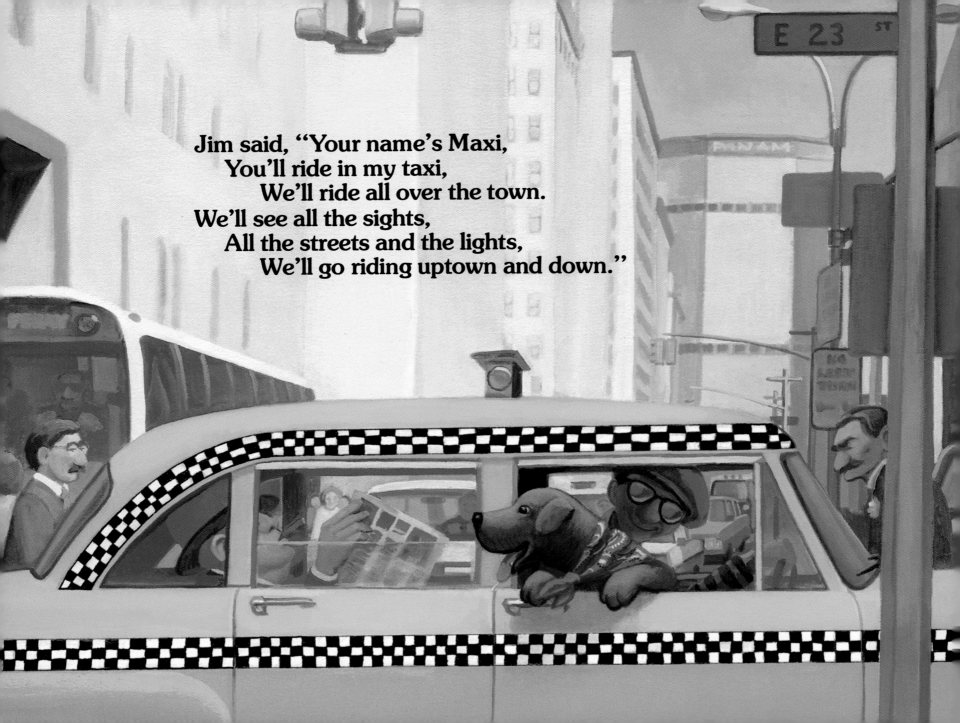

Jim said, "Your name's Maxi,
You'll ride in my taxi,
We'll ride all over the town.
We'll see all the sights,
All the streets and the lights,
We'll go riding uptown and down."

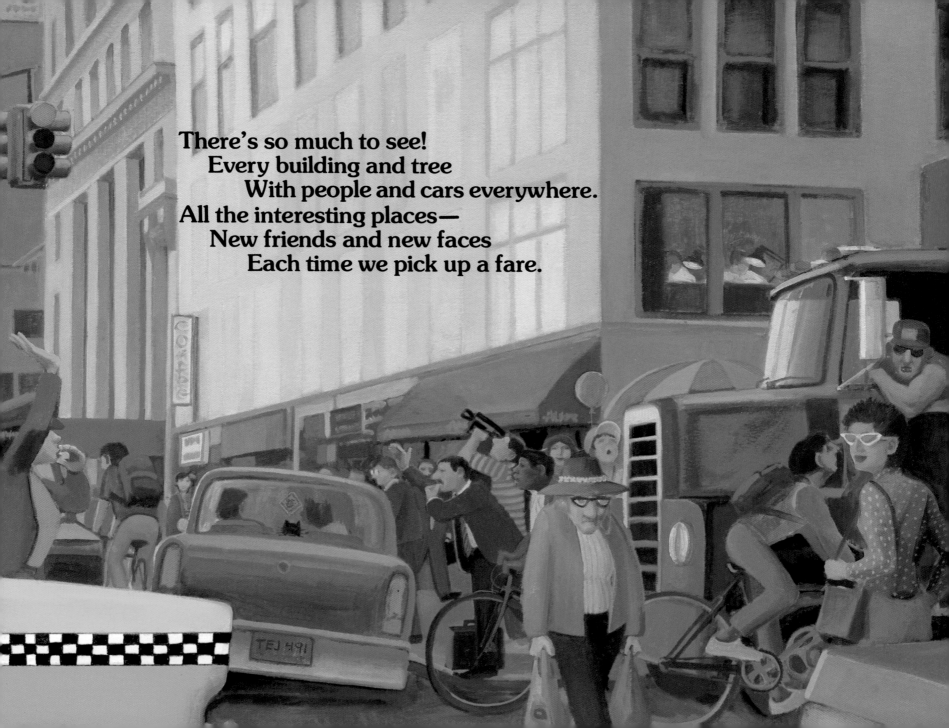

There's so much to see!
Every building and tree
With people and cars everywhere.
All the interesting places—
New friends and new faces
Each time we pick up a fare.

One time a big lady
   Who said she was Sadie
      Was singing that night in a show.
She broke into a song
   And I sang right along—
      You couldn't tell me from the pro!

"To the hospital, quick!
    My wife is quite sick,"
        Cried a man as we stopped for the light,
"Our baby is due!"
    And like lightning we flew—
        We made it in time—what a night!

Sometimes when it's slow
  To the airport we go.
      We get in the line at the stand
To wait for a fare,
  And a hotdog we share
      While we watch the planes take off and land.

The door opened wide—
　　Guess who jumped inside?
　　　　Two clowns and a chimp they called Murray!
"We're performing at eight
　　And our flight came in late—
　　　　To the circus, and please try to hurry!"

We get such big tips
　　On most of our trips—
　　　　Jim is surprised at this treat.
But he doesn't know
　　That I put on a show
　　　　For the passengers in the backseat!

At the end of each day
When we've earned our pay,
We drive the cab back to its spot,
Where our boss named Lou
Says, "Hi! How'd ya do?
Have a biscuit!" (He likes me a lot.)

It's just like a dream,
  Me and Jim—we're a team!
   I'm always there at his side.
We never stand still,
  Every day's a new thrill—
   Come join us next time for a ride!

ABOUT THE AUTHORS

Debra and Sal Barracca work with many artists and writers of children's books
through their young company, Halcyon Books.
Both are native New Yorkers and they were inspired to write
The Adventures of Taxi Dog after riding in a taxi whose owner kept his dog
with him in the front seat. They will donate a portion of the book's
proceeds to The Fund for Animals in New York City.
The Barraccas live in Croton-on-Hudson, New York with their three cats.

ABOUT THE ARTIST

Mark Buehner grew up in Utah and graduated from Utah State University.
Mr. Buehner works as a freelance illustrator and
The Adventures of Taxi Dog is his first book. He now lives with
his wife and two children in Brooklyn, New York.